To Uncle Don, my favorite marine —P.M.

To my wife, Francesca, the good sergeant of my life —I.B.

Balzer + Bray is an imprint of HarperCollins Publishers.

Sergeant Reckless: The True Story of the Little Horse Who Became a Hero
Text copyright © 2017 by Patricia McCormick
Illustrations copyright © 2017 by Iacopo Bruno

Library of Congress Control Number: 2016950249
ISBN 978-0-06-229259-9

The illustrations for this book were drawn with pencil and colored digitally.
Typography by Iacopo Bruno and Amy Ryan
18 19 20 21 PC 10 9 8 7 6 5 4

First Edition

SERGEANT Reckless

THE TRUE STORY OF THE LITTLE HORSE WHO BECAME A HERO

WRITTEN BY
Patricia McCormick

ILLUSTRATED BY
Iacopo Bruno

BALZER + BRAY
An Imprint of HarperCollins Publishers

STARS *PACIFIC AND* STRIPES EXTRA!

VOLUME 6. NUMBER 149   SUNDAY. June 25. 1950   SHARE THIS PAPER

KOREA AT WAR

The small red mare whinnied for her supper. But Korea was at war. Towns were shattered. Fields were scorched. And the racetrack was abandoned. No one paid attention to the hungry little horse.

Nearby, U.S. Marines were exhausted from hauling heavy ammunition uphill to a powerful new cannon nicknamed the "reckless" rifle. That's when their leader, Lt. Eric Pedersen, had an idea. What if he could get a mule to carry the shells?

But all Lt. Pedersen could find was a scrawny sorrel mare with a white blaze and three matching socks. She wasn't much, but she reminded him of a horse he'd had as a boy, so he took a chance on her.

FM 23-11

DEPARTMENT OF THE ARMY FIELD MANUAL

75MM RECOILLESS RIFLE, M20

RECKLESS ★ RIFLE

This copy is a reprint which includes current changes in force — C 2 and C 3. These changes are located at the back of this publication.

HEADQUARTERS, DEPARTMENT OF
JULY 1950

Back at the base, as the marines gathered around to meet the new recruit, Lt. Pedersen realized he'd forgotten to buy hay. One of the men held out a piece of bread. The mare gobbled it up.

Then she devoured the rest of the loaf. Another man offered her some oatmeal. She licked the bowl clean.

the United States of America

She was pretty, the marines agreed, but she was small. How could she carry such heavy ammunition? And how would she react when she heard the thunder of the cannon? A mule was slow and steady, but a racehorse was high-strung and skittish. She'd have to go through special training—and she'd start out at the same rank as any newbie: private. Private Reckless.

The first thing Pvt. Reckless had to learn was to duck incoming fire. Which meant that her trainer, Sgt. Joseph Latham, had to teach her to kneel down. First, he gave her a sugar cube every time he tapped her front leg. Then another one when she knelt down. Before long, the greedy little horse knelt down the moment he tapped her leg.

Reckless also had to learn to retreat. When Latham gave the command, she had to trot back to her bunker, where another reward was waiting.

An apple. Or a chocolate candy bar. Or a peanut butter sandwich. Even a can of beans. Whatever it was, Reckless ate it.

Next, Latham led her up the hill to the cannon. With a little coaxing—and a lot of chocolate— she'd soon follow Latham anywhere.

Finally, she was fitted with a packsaddle—a padded wooden cargo frame with leather straps across her chest and legs. Unlike a racing saddle, it was big, bulky, and constricting.

LATHAM
cinched up the girth and the men stood back, expecting her to try to throw it off.

RECKLESS
just stood there.

They loaded ammunition shells onto her pack— and waited for her to buck. But she just put her head down and marched up the hill.

Her reward that day was . . .

AN ICE-COLD
COCA-COLA

By now, Reckless thought of herself as a member of the company and was free to roam the camp. One morning she showed up at the mess hall, where the cook gave her an apple. She nudged his shoulder for more, so he offered her scrambled eggs and toast. From then on, she ate the same breakfast as the men— and washed it down with a cup of coffee.

— TODAY —

CHICKEN CARBONARA

— TORTILLAS —

12 MEALS C

WT 25 CU 1.31

89

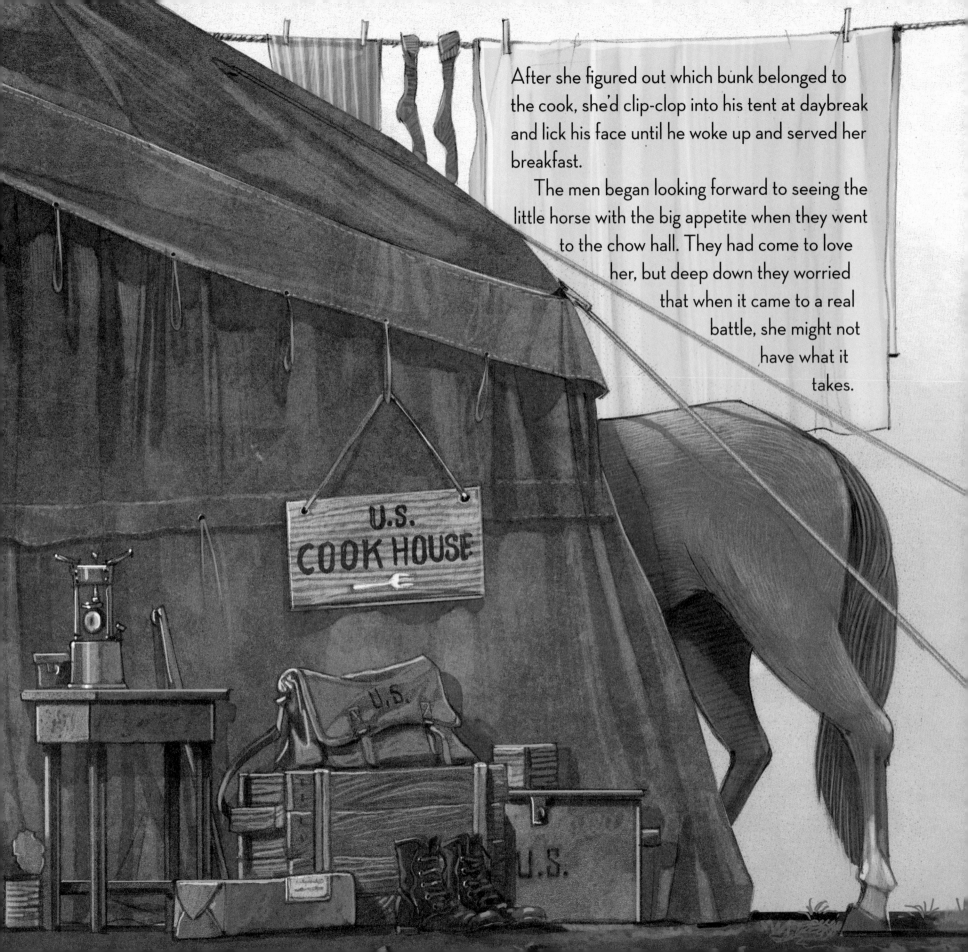

After she figured out which bunk belonged to the cook, she'd clip-clop into his tent at daybreak and lick his face until he woke up and served her breakfast.

The men began looking forward to seeing the little horse with the big appetite when they went to the chow hall. They had come to love her, but deep down they worried that when it came to a real battle, she might not have what it takes.

U.S.
COOK HOUSE

U.S.

U.S.

One day, the marines spotted enemy troops approaching; instantly, they went into battle mode. Pvt. Monroe Coleman saddled up Reckless and led her to the top of the hill.

BOOM!

Just as they were delivering their load, the cannon went off. A blast of hot air sent dust and gravel flying toward the horse. Reckless jumped straight in the air—even with six shells on her back.

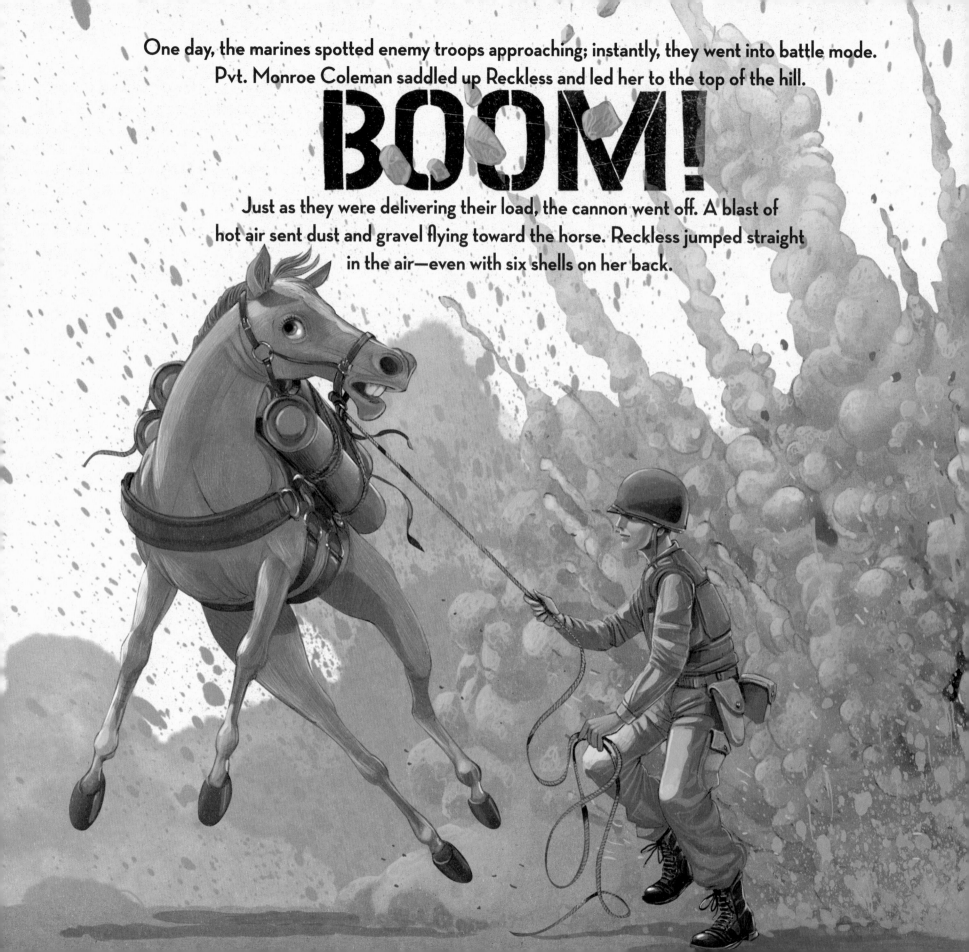

"Easy, girl," Coleman said, stroking her mane.

BOOM!

The cannon roared again. She jumped, but not so high this time.

BOOM!

This time, Reckless just snorted. By the next time the gun went off, Reckless was busy eating a helmet liner she'd found in the grass.

From then on, Reckless was one of the guys. On cold nights, she snuck into Latham's tent and slept on the floor. And when the men played poker, she joined in. One night, she'd eaten about thirty dollars' worth of poker chips before they caught on.

SERVICE
de Luxe
PLAYING CARDS
★

MADE IN U.S.A.

MADE IN U.S.A.

Reckless served in more skirmishes, but her most dangerous assignment came at the Battle of Outpost Vegas. That night, the men awoke to shells and white-hot flares falling right inside the base. Reckless trotted back to her bunker, trembling. And for the first time, she refused to eat.

But the minute she was loaded with her pack, Reckless got to work.

At the base of the path, she took a deep breath, pricked her ears forward, and charged the hill.

Without a word of urging, she broke into a trot and then a gallop. The heavy shells banged against her sides as she hit the steep incline. The first rays of dawn were lighting the sky as she arrived at the top of the trail, her flanks heaving.

The sky was full of smoke. Shells whizzed by and cannons boomed. All day, Reckless marched up and down the windy path—hauling her load. As she passed her fellow marines along the way, they gave her their chocolate bars to keep up her strength.

CONTROL No. 1012

KEEP THIS KIT FILLED

FIRST AID KIT

FOR EMERGENCY USE ONLY

INSTRUCTIONS

12-UNIT KIT

Then a piece of shrapnel hit Reckless over her left eye. Blood trickled down onto her white blaze, but she kept going. Later, another piece of shrapnel hit her left flank. After a dab of iodine and a drink of water, she was back at work.

Night fell as sizzling flares cast eerie shadows on the landscape. The marines were beginning to tire. But they saw the little mare silhouetted on the ridge, her head hanging as she put everything she had into her job.

She was soaked in sweat, lather curling up over her saddle. When she came back down the hill, one by one the men took off their body-armor jackets and laid them over her for protection.

STOCK NO.
PETROLATUM

STOCK NO. 1
AMMONIA

STOCK NO.
TOURNIQUE

STOCK NO
FIRST AID

STOCK N
BAND
EACH

STOCK N
BAND
4 x 4 INS

STOCK NO
BAND
DYED DR

STOCK N
BAND

By the end of the day, Reckless had:

☑ made fifty-one trips

☑ gone a distance of thirty-five miles up and down steep terrain

☑ carried nine thousand pounds of ammunition

That battle helped change the course of the war.

At last, there was a cease-fire, and
Reckless was able to rest. The marines
promoted Reckless to sergeant, and then
they came, one by one, to say good-bye
to the little mare who'd shown as much
heart on the battlefield as any man
among them.

When they got home, they
started a campaign to bring
Reckless to the United States.

A ship owner agreed to pay her passage and the men took up a collection to buy her a beautiful scarlet-and-gold blanket with sergeant's stripes. But by the time the boat arrived, Reckless had eaten her blanket—ribbons and all!

Sgt. Reckless, the little mare who became a marine, is the only animal to officially hold military rank. She received two Purple Hearts and retired with full military honors and the rank of staff sergeant.

Her story is a testament to the mysterious bond between humans and animals and proof of the Marine Corps motto: *Semper Fidelis.* Ever faithful.

AUTHOR'S NOTE

SELECTED BIBLIOGRAPHY

Greer, Andrew. *Reckless: Pride of the Marines*. New Y
E. P. Dutton, 1955.

Hoffman, Nancy Lee White. "Sgt. Reckless: Combat
Veteran." *Leatherneck* magazine, November 1992

The Korean War started in 1950 when troops from the north crossed the dividing line between Communist-backed North Korea and American-backed South Korea. The fighting went on for three years, and Americans were concerned that a wider war with the Soviet Union or China would erupt, setting off a possible third world war. Finally, after nearly five million military and civilian deaths, the fighting ceased. No peace treaty was ever signed, and the Korean peninsula is still divided today.

I first learned about Sgt. Reckless from a Veterans Day article in the *New York Times* featuring the cook from the Fifth Marine Regiment Anti-Tank Company. It turned out that Sgt. John T. Meyers, who made Reckless her morning coffee and eggs, lived not far from me and was happy to talk about the little horse who ate everything in sight. In the mornings, she poked her head into his tent and licked him until he woke up. Then she would follow him to the mess hall.

While Sgt. Reckless was famous for her appetite, it was her heroism on the battlefield that made her a legend. In one battle, she rescued a group of men who were pinned down by enemy fire, allowing them to escape as she shielded them. Later, she carried wounded marines from the hill.

Reckless displayed her fearlessness and big heart early on. She was originally owned by a Korean boy, Kim Huk Moon, who named her Flame because of her reddish coat and fiery speed on the racetrack. But when war broke out in Seoul, Kim had to flee, hitching Flame to a cart filled with his family's belongings.

Sgt. Jo